ADHD isn't ME!

CANDACE CURRY

To order additional copies of this book, contact:
Xlibris
844-714-8691
www.Xlibris.com
Orders@Xlibris.com

ISBN: Softcover   978-1-6641-9166-2
        EBook   978-1-6641-9165-5

Print information available on the last page

Rev. date: 09/16/2021

For Ciera, the little girl with SUPER POWERS!
Mommy loves you to the moon and back,
forever and always. Keep on being SUPER.
— CC

So recently my Mommy took me to the Doctor
and he told me that I have **ADHD**...
but I said "**ADHD** isn't me!"
Actually....

The truth is that I have many **SUPER POWERS** that many people just don't understand.

SUPER POWER 1

People say that I am **LOUD**,
But I just have a lot to say.
I have the **SUPER POWER** to
SPEAK LOUD.

SUPER POWER 2

My Teacher tells me to focus.
But I am focused.
Focused on everything around me.
Even the things that most people overlook, like
the beautiful bow that I found in my desk,
The cracks in the walls, and the
squiggly shape of my fingernail.
That is my **SUPER POWER**... Focus!

SUPER POWER 3

I am full of excitement.
I love to share it with
Everyone around Me.
That's my **SUPER POWER**
The Power to Cheer You Up!

SUPER POWER 4

I have a billion thoughts in my mind.
I don't want to be stingy
By keeping MY Thoughts all to myself.
So I talk about them until they are all out.
My thoughts never run out.
That is my **SUPER POWER**
MY voice...My power to speak!

SUPER POWER 5

Sitting in one place is **SO not Me.**
I like to Move and Groove
I like to move it like the song
From my favorite movie "**Madagascar**"
That is my move it **SUPER POWER.**

SUPER POWER 6

My last **SUPER POWER** is my all time favorite...
It's the power to make sound.
All the best videos and movies have sound and so do I.
Sometimes the sounds are dancing around having a
party in my mind but sometimes they spill out.
I try not to let them spill out because people without my
powers let things quiet...but quiet is **BORRIINNGG!!**
I have my own **SOUND EFFECTS-**
That's my **SUPER POWER!**

My Mommy tells me that everyone is
different and that makes us special.
So my **SUPER POWERS** make me **SUPER SPECIAL**.

What is Your **Super POWER?**

ADHD Facts

ADHD stands for Attention- Deficit Hyperactivity Disorder.

<u>**ADHD is real.**</u> It is caused by differences in the brain. Merely "trying harder to focus" doesn't make it easier or even possible. Millions of children and adults have ADHD.

Women and girls are diagnosed as frequently as men and boys.

Some people with ADHD are "day dreamers" while others are "overly active or hyper."

ADHD effects executive functions or the ability to successfully execute or complete tasks.

ADHD isn't caused by laziness or a lack of discipline.

ADHD can be a strength. Many people who have been diagnosed with ADHD are highly creative and "outside of the box" thinkers.

About the Author:

The author of this book is my real life Mommy, her name is **Candace Curry**. She always makes me feel **SUPER!**

Candace Curry, was born and raised in Brooklyn New York where she continues to reside with her family. She is a mother, a Teacher, an entrepreneur and the wearer of many, many hats but the one that she cherishes most is that of mother to her two young daughters.

Printed in the United States
by Baker & Taylor Publisher Services